MY 1ST GRAPHIC NOVEL®

The Lost LUNCH

MY FIRST GRAPHIC NOVELS ARE PUBLISHED BY STONE ARCH BOOKS
A CAPSTONE IMPRINT
1710 ROE CREST DRIVE
NORTH MANKATO, MINNESOTA 56003
WWW.CAPSTONEPUB.COM

Library of Congress Cataloging-in-Publication data is available on the Library of Congress website.

ISBN-13: 978-1-4342-2014-1 (library binding)
ISBN-13: 978-1-4342-3103-1 (paperback)

Summary: When Andrew's lunch goes missing, he is left sad and hungry. With the help of his friend Dylan, the search for the lost lunch begins!

Art Director: BOB LENTZ
Graphic Designer: EMILY HARRIS
Production Specialist: MICHELLE BIEDSCHEID

The Lost LUNCH

by Lori Mortensen

illustrated by Rémy Simard

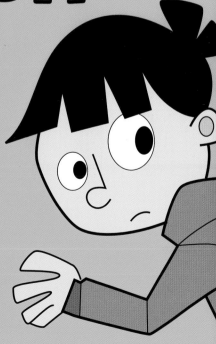

STONE ARCH BOOKS
a capstone imprint

How To Read
A GRAPHIC NOVEL

Graphic novels are easy to read. Boxes called panels show you how to follow the story. Look at the panels from left to right and top to bottom.

Read the word boxes and word balloons from left to right as well. Don't forget the sound and action words in the pictures.

The pictures and the words work together to tell the whole story.

Andrew and Dylan arrived at school early.

Andrew put down his lunch and his backpack.

Andrew and Dylan started on the swings.

Then they played on the slide.

They finished with the monkey bars.

Then the bell rang.

Andrew grabbed his backpack and went to class.

He took a spelling test. He finished his reading.

He worked on his math problems. Soon, it was time for lunch.

Andrew and his class walked to the cafeteria.

The hamburgers smelled great.

Suddenly, Andrew stopped.

Andrew told his teacher.

Andrew hurried back to the classroom and looked in his desk.

His lunch wasn't there.

Andrew returned to the cafeteria and sat next to Dylan.

But by then, all that was left was a pickle.

During recess, Andrew thought about his lunch.

Andrew raced to where he'd dropped his lunch before school.

Andrew and Dylan searched the swings.

They searched the slide.

They searched the monkey bars.

They couldn't find Andrew's lunch anywhere.

Andrew sat on a bench. His stomach growled.
Soon recess would be over.

Andrew would be hungry all day!

Andrew ran toward the school.

Andrew raced to the main office. He stopped at the front desk.

She held up a brown bag.

The lost lunch was no longer lost.

The End

About the AUTHOR

Lori Mortensen is a multi-published children's author who writes fiction and nonfiction on all sorts of subjects. When she's not plunking away at the keyboard, she enjoys making cheesy bread rolls, gardening, and hanging out with her family at their home in northern California.

About the ILLUSTRATOR

Rémy Simard began his career as an illustrator in 1980. Today he creates computer-generated illustrations for a large variety of clients. He has also written and illustrated more than 30 children's books in both French and English, including *Monsieur Noir et Blanc*, a finalist for Canada's Governor's Prize. To relax, Rémy likes to race around on his motorcycle. Rémy resides in Montreal with his two sons and a cat named Billy.

GLOSSARY

CAFETERIA (kaf-uh-TIHR-ee-uh) — a place to eat

GROWLED (GROULD) — a rumbling noise that comes from your stomach

RECESS (REE-sess) — a break from schoolwork

SEARCHED (SURCHD) — looked for something

STARVING (STARV-ing) — very hungry

DISCUSSION QUESTIONS

1. What is your favorite school lunch? Why?

2. Andrew and Dylan do a lot of things together. What do you and your friends like to do together?

3. What would you do if you lost your lunch?

WRITING PROMPTS

1. The lunchroom can be a crazy place. Make a list of at least three lunchroom rules.

2. Do you like breakfast, lunch, or dinner best? Write a paragraph about your favorite meal of the day.

3. Think about a time that you lost something. Write a paragraph describing what you lost. Did you ever find the missing item?

The First Step into GRAPHIC NOVELS

These books are the perfect introduction to the world of safe, appealing graphic novels. Each story uses familiar topics, repeating patterns, and core vocabulary words appropriate for a beginning reader. Combine the entertaining story with comic book panels, exciting action elements, and bright colors and a safe graphic novel is born.

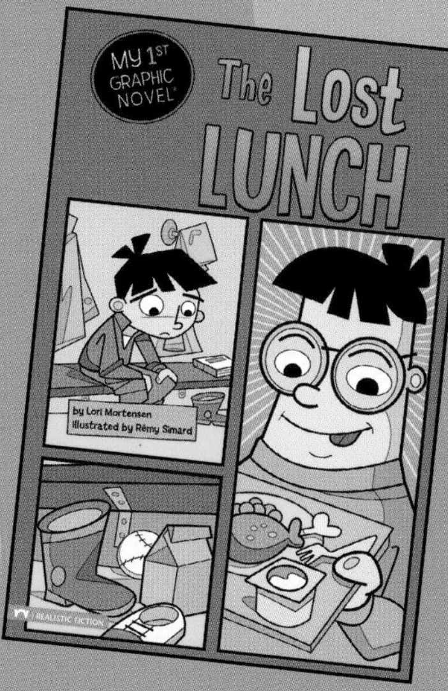
MY 1ST GRAPHIC NOVEL
The Lost LUNCH
by Lori Mortensen
illustrated by Rémy Simard
REALISTIC FICTION

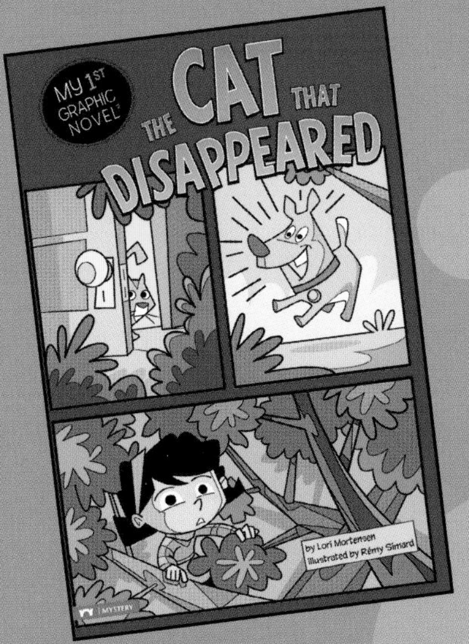
MY 1ST GRAPHIC NOVEL
THE CAT THAT DISAPPEARED
by Lori Mortensen
illustrated by Rémy Simard
MYSTERY

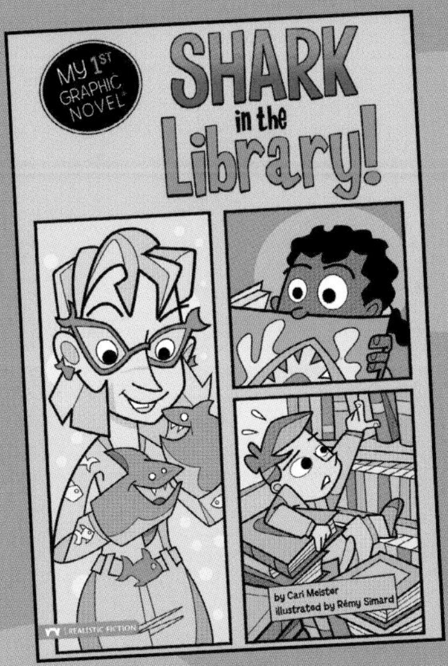
MY 1ST GRAPHIC NOVEL
SHARK in the Library!
by Cari Meister
illustrated by Rémy Simard
REALISTIC FICTION

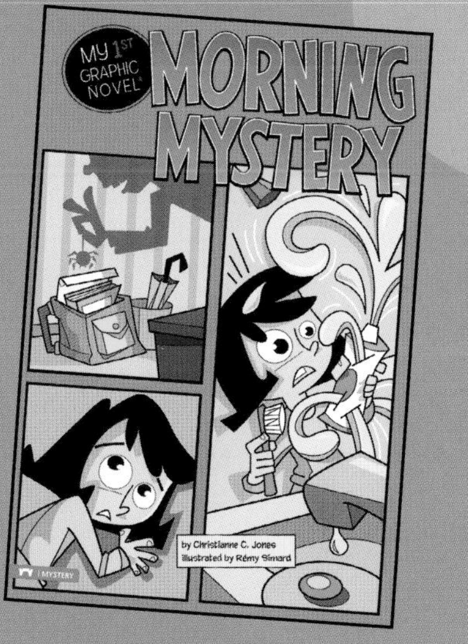
MY 1ST GRAPHIC NOVEL
MORNING MYSTERY
by Christianne C. Jones
illustrated by Rémy Simard
MYSTERY

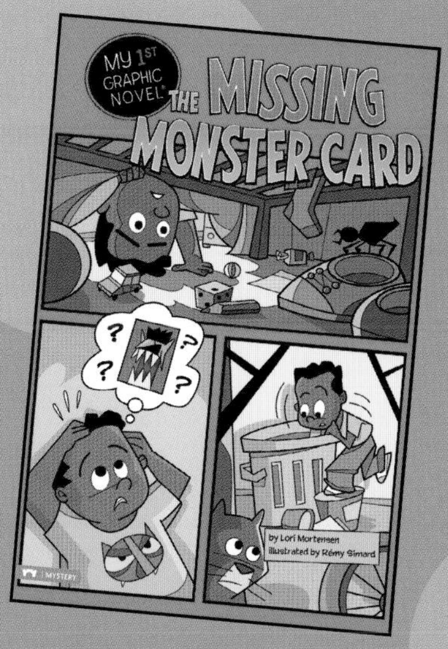
MY 1ST GRAPHIC NOVEL
THE MISSING MONSTER CARD
by Lori Mortensen
illustrated by Rémy Simard
MYSTERY

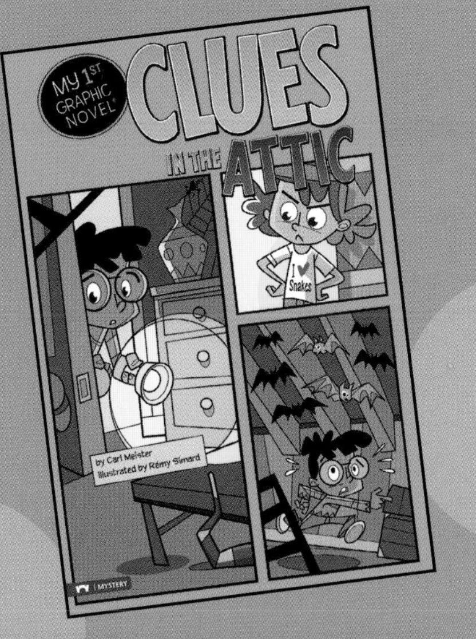
MY 1ST GRAPHIC NOVEL
CLUES IN THE ATTIC
I ♥ Snakes
by Cari Meister
illustrated by Rémy Simard
MYSTERY

WAIT!

DON'T CLOSE THE BOOK!

capstone
kids
.com

THERE'S MORE!

FIND MORE:

Games & Puzzles
Heroes & Villains
Authors & Illustrators

AT...

www.CAPSTONEKIDS.com